CONTENTS

ALFIE
GETS IN FIRST

One day Alfie and Mom and Annie Rose were coming home from shopping. Alfie ran on ahead, because he wanted to get home first. He ran all the way from the corner to the front gate and up the steps to the front door.

Then he sat down on the top step and waited for the others. Along came Mom, pushing Annie Rose and the groceries.

"I raced you!" called Alfie. "I'm back first, so there!"

Annie Rose didn't care. She was tired. She sat back in her stroller and sucked her thumb.

Mom put the brake on the stroller and
left Annie Rose at the bottom of the steps
while she lifted the basket of groceries up to
the top. Then she found the key and opened
the front door. Alfie dashed in ahead of her.

"I've won! I've won!" he shouted.

Mom put the basket down in the hall and
went back down the steps to lift Annie Rose
out of her stroller. But what do you think
Alfie did then?

He gave the door a great big slam—BANG!
—just like that.

Then Mom was outside the door, holding
Annie Rose, and Alfie was inside with the
groceries. Mom's key was inside too.

14

"Open the door, Alfie," said Mom.

But Alfie didn't know how to open the door from the inside. The catch was too high up. Mom looked into the mail slot.

"Try to reach the catch and turn it," she said. Alfie tried, but he couldn't quite reach it.

"Can you put the key through the mail slot?" asked Mom. But Alfie couldn't reach the mail slot either.

Annie Rose was hungry as well as tired. She began to cry. Then Alfie began to cry too. He didn't like being all by himself on the other side of the door. Just then Mrs. MacNally came hurrying across the street to see what all the noise was about.

She and Mom said encouraging things
into the mail slot.

But Alfie still couldn't open the door.

"Go and get your little chair from the living room, and then you'll be able to reach the catch," said Mom. But Alfie didn't try to get his little chair. He just went on crying, louder and louder, and Annie Rose cried louder and louder too.

"There's my Maureen," said Mrs. MacNally. "I'm sure she'll be able to help."

Mrs. MacNally's Maureen was a big girl. Right away she came and joined Mom and Annie Rose and Mrs. MacNally on the top step.

"Mmm, might have to break a window," she said. "But I'll try to climb up the drainpipe first, if you like."

But Mrs. MacNally didn't like that idea at all.

"Oh, no, Maureen, you might hurt yourself," she said.

Just then Alfie's very good friend the milkman came up the street in his milk truck.

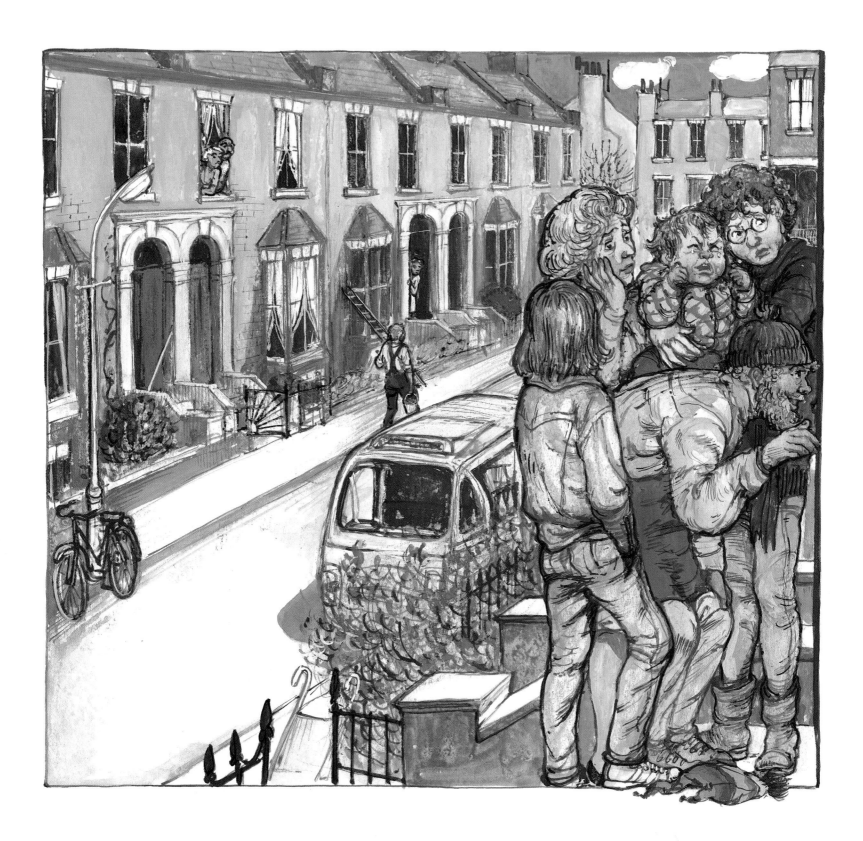

When he saw Mom and Annie Rose and Mrs.
MacNally and Mrs. MacNally's Maureen all standing
on the top step, he stopped his truck and said, "What's
the trouble?"

So they told him.

"Don't worry, mate," the milkman shouted. "We'll
soon have you out of there."

"Mmm, looks as though this lock's going to be difficult to break," said the milkman.

But then Mrs. MacNally's Maureen had a very good idea. She ran to ask the window cleaner, who was working up the street, if he would bring his ladder and climb up to the bathroom window. And, of course, when the window cleaner heard about Alfie, he came hurrying along with his ladder as quickly as he could.

Then Mom and Annie Rose and Mrs. MacNally and Mrs. MacNally's Maureen and the milkman all stood on the top step and watched while the window cleaner put his ladder up against the house. He started to climb up to the bathroom window. But when he was halfway up the ladder, what do you think happened?

The front door suddenly opened, and there was Alfie! He had managed to reach the catch and turn it—like that—after all.

He was *very* pleased with himself.

He opened the front door as wide as it would go and stood back grandly to let everybody in.

Then the window cleaner came down from his
ladder, and he and the milkman and Mrs. MacNally's
Maureen and Mrs. MacNally and Annie Rose and Mom
and Alfie all went into the kitchen and had tea together.

ALFIE'S FEET

This little pig went to market,

This little pig stayed at home,

This little pig had roast beef,

This little pig had none,

And this little pig cried,

Wee-wee-wee,

All the way home.

Alfie had a little sister called Annie Rose.
Alfie's feet were quite big. Annie Rose's feet
were rather small. They were all soft and pink
underneath. Alfie knew a game he could play
with Annie Rose, counting her toes.

Annie Rose had lots of different ways of getting around. She went forward, crawling,

and backward, on her behind,

and she liked to slide about very fast on her potty,

skidding around and around
on the floor and in and out
of the table legs.

Annie Rose had
some new red shoes.

She could walk in them
a little, if she was pushing
her cart or holding on to
someone's hand.

When they went out, Annie Rose wore her
red shoes, and Alfie wore his old brown ones.
Mom usually helped him put them on, because
he wasn't very good at tying the laces yet.

42

If it had been raining, Alfie
liked to go stamping in mud
and walking through puddles,

splish, splash, SPLOSH!

43

Then his shoes got pretty wet.

So did his socks,

and so did his feet.

So one Saturday morning Alfie and Mom went to
a big store on Main Street.

They bought a pair of shiny new yellow boots for Alfie to wear when he went stamping in mud and walking through puddles. Alfie was very pleased. He carried them home himself in a cardboard box.

50

When they got home, Alfie sat down at once and unwrapped his new boots. He put them on all by himself and walked around in them.

Stamp! Stamp! Stamp!

He went into the kitchen to show Mom and Dad and Annie Rose, stamping his feet all the way.

Stamp! Stamp! Stamp!

The boots were very bright
and shiny, but they felt funny.

Alfie wanted to go out again right away. So he put on his jacket, and Dad took his book and his newspaper, and they went off to the park.

Alfie stamped in a lot of mud and walked through a lot of puddles, splish, splash, SPLOSH! He frightened some sparrows who were having a bath. He even frightened two big ducks. They went hurrying back to their pond, walking with their feet turned in.

Alfie looked down at his feet. They still
felt funny. They kept turning outward.
Dad was sitting on a bench. They both
looked at Alfie's feet.

Suddenly Alfie knew what was wrong!

Dad lifted Alfie onto the bench beside him and helped him to take off each boot and put it on the other foot. And when Alfie stood up again, his feet didn't feel a bit funny anymore.

After lunch Mom painted a big black *R* on one of Alfie's boots and a big black *L* on the other to help Alfie remember which boot was which. The *R* was for *Right foot* and the *L* was for *Left foot*. The black paint wore off after a while, and the boots stopped being new and shiny, but Alfie usually did remember to get them on the correct feet after that. They felt much better when he went stamping in mud and walking through puddles.

And, of course, Annie Rose made such a fuss about Alfie having new boots that she had to have a pair of her own to go stamping around in too, splish, splash, SPLOSH!

ALFIE
GIVES A HAND

One day Alfie came home from nursery
school with a card in an envelope. His best
friend, Bernard, had given it to him.

"Look, it's got my name on it," said
Alfie, pointing.

"It's an invitation to Bernard's birthday
party," said Mom.

"Will it be at Bernard's house?" Alfie wanted to know. He'd never been there before. Mom said yes, and she told him all about birthday parties and how you had to take a present, and about the games and how there would be nice things to eat.

Alfie was very excited about Bernard's party. When the day came, Mom washed Alfie's face and brushed his hair and helped him put on a clean T-shirt and his brand-new shorts.

71

"You and Annie Rose are going to be at the party too, aren't you?" asked Alfie.

"Oh, no," said Mom. "I'll take you to Bernard's house, and then Annie Rose and I will go to the park and come back to collect you when it's time to go home."

"But I want you to be there," said Alfie.

Mom told him that she and Annie Rose hadn't been invited to the party, only Alfie, because he was Bernard's special friend.

"You don't mind my leaving you at nursery school, do you?" she said. "So you won't mind being at Bernard's house either, as soon as you get there."

Mom had bought some crayons for Alfie to give Bernard for his birthday present. While she was wrapping them up, Alfie went upstairs. He looked under his pillow and found his old bit of blanket, which he kept in bed with him at night.

He brought it downstairs and sat down to wait for Mom.

"You won't want your old blanket at the party," said Mom when it was time to go.

But Alfie wouldn't leave his blanket behind. He held it tightly with one hand, and Bernard's present with the other, all the way to Bernard's house.

When they got there, Bernard's mom opened the door.
"Hello, Alfie," she said. "Let's go into the yard and
find Bernard and the others."
Then Mom gave Alfie a kiss and said good-bye
and went off to the park with Annie Rose.

"Would you like to put your blanket down here with the coats?" asked Bernard's mom. But Alfie didn't want to put his blanket down. He still held on to it very tightly.

Bernard was in the garden with Min and Sam and Daniel and some other children from the nursery school.

"Happy birthday!" Alfie remembered to say, and he gave Bernard his present. Bernard pulled off the paper.

"Crayons! How lovely!" said Bernard's mom. "Say thank you, Bernard."

"Thank you," said Bernard. But do you know what he did then?

He threw the crayons up in the air. They landed all
over the grass.

"That was a silly thing to do," said Bernard's mom
as she picked up the crayons and put them away.

Then Bernard's mom brought out some bubble stuff and blew lots of bubbles into the air. They floated all over the yard, and the children jumped around, trying to pop them.

Alfie couldn't pop many bubbles, because he was holding on to his blanket. But Bernard jumped around and pushed and popped more bubbles than anyone else.

"Don't push people, Bernard," said Bernard's mom sternly.

One huge bubble landed lightly on Min's sleeve. It stayed there, quivering and shiny. Min smiled. She stood very still.

Then Bernard came up behind her and popped the big bubble.

Min began to cry. Bernard's mom was cross with Bernard and told him to say he was sorry.

"Never mind, we're going to have something to eat now, dear," she told Min. "Who would you like to sit next to?"

Min wanted to sit next to Alfie. She stopped crying and pulled her chair right up close to his.

On the table there were sandwiches and little hot dogs and potato chips and Jell-O and a big cake with candles and "Happy Birthday, Bernard" written on it.

Bernard took a huge breath and blew out
all the candles at once—*Phoooooo!* Everyone
clapped and sang, "Happy birthday to you."

Then Bernard blew into his lemonade through his straw and made rude bubbling noises. He blew into his Jell-O too until his mom took it away from him.

Alfie liked everything . . . but holding on to his blanket made eating rather difficult. It got all mixed up with the Jell-O and potato chips and covered in sticky crumbs.

When they'd finished eating, Bernard's mom said that they were all going to play a game. But Bernard ran off and fetched his very best present. It was a tiger mask.

Bernard went behind a bush and came out wearing the mask and making terrible growling noises: "Grrr! Grrr, grrrr, GRRRR! ACHT!"

He went crawling around the yard,
sounding very fierce and frightening.
    Min began to cry again. She clung to
Alfie.

"Get up *at once,* Bernard," said Bernard's mom. "It's not that kind of game. Now let's all stand in a circle, everyone, and join hands."

Bernard stopped growling, but he wouldn't take off his tiger mask. Instead, he grabbed Alfie's hand to pull him into the circle.

Bernard's mom tried to take Min's hand and bring her into the circle too. But Min wouldn't hold anyone's hand but Alfie's. She went on crying. She cried and cried.

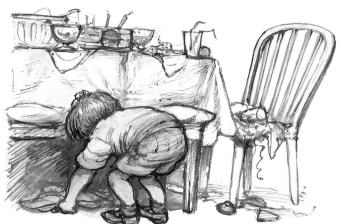

Then Alfie made a brave decision. He ran and put down his blanket, very carefully, in a safe place underneath the table.

Now he could hold Min's hand too, as well as Bernard's.

Min stopped crying. She wasn't
frightened of Bernard in his tiger mask
now that she was holding Alfie's hand.

She joined in the game, and they all
danced around together, singing:

"Ring-a-ring-o'-roses
A pocket full of posies
A-tishoo, a-tishoo,
We all fall DOWN!"

Afterward Alfie and Min joined in with some more games and ate ice cream and popcorn and bounced balloons with the others. Alfie had such a good time that his blanket stayed under the table until Mom and Annie Rose came to collect him.

"What a helpful guest you've been, Alfie," said Bernard's mom when Alfie thanked her and said good-bye. "Min wouldn't have enjoyed the party a bit without you. I *do* wish Bernard would learn to be helpful sometimes—

Perhaps he will, one day."

On the way home, Alfie carried his blanket in one hand and a balloon and a bag of candy in the other. His blanket looked a bit messy, and it *had* been in the way. Next time, he thought, he might leave it safely at home, after all.

AN EVENING
AT ALFIE'S

One cold winter evening . . .

Alfie and his little sister, Annie Rose, were
ready for bed,

Mom and Dad were ready to go out,

and the MacNallys' daughter, Maureen, was in the living room. She had come to look after Alfie and Annie Rose while Mom and Dad went to a party.

Alfie and Maureen waved good-bye from the window.

Annie Rose was already in her crib. Soon she settled down and went to sleep.

Alfie liked Maureen. She always read him a
story when she came to baby-sit.

106

Tonight Alfie wanted the story about Noah and his ark full of animals. Alfie liked to hear how the rain came drip, drip, drip, and then splash! splash! splash! and then rushing everywhere, until the whole world was covered with water.

When Maureen had finished the story, it was time for Alfie to go to bed. She came upstairs to tuck him in. They had to be very quiet and talk in whispers so they wouldn't wake up Annie Rose.

Maureen gave Alfie a good-night hug and went downstairs, leaving the door a little bit open.

Alfie didn't feel sleepy. He lay in bed,
looking at the patch of light on the ceiling. For
a long time all was quiet. Then he heard a
funny noise outside in the hall.

Alfie sat up. The noise was just outside his door. Drip, drip, drip! Soon it got quicker. It changed to drip-drip, drip-drip, drip-drip! It was getting louder too.

Alfie got out of bed and peeped around the door. There was a puddle on the floor. He looked up. Water was splashing into the puddle from the ceiling, drip-drip, drip-drip, drip-drip! It was raining inside the house!

Alfie went downstairs. Maureen was doing
her homework in front of the television.
"It's raining upstairs," Alfie told her.

Alfie and Maureen went up to look. The puddle was getting bigger. The drip-drip, drip-drip, drip-drip had turned into a splash! splash! splash!

"Hmm, looks like a burst pipe," said Maureen. A plumber was one of the things she wanted to be when she left school.

"Better get a bucket," she said. So Alfie showed her where the bucket was kept, in the kitchen cupboard with the brushes and brooms.

But now the water was
dripping down in another
place. Alfie and Maureen
found two of Mom's big
mixing bowls and put them
underneath the drips.

Maureen got on the telephone to her mother. The MacNallys lived just across the street. Mrs. MacNally was there in a moment.

"Oh, dear, oh, dear, it's ruining your mother's floor!" cried Mrs. MacNally. "Fetch some towels, Maureen!"

Just then Annie Rose woke up and began to cry.
"Shh, shh, there, there," said Mrs. MacNally,
bending over her crib. But Annie Rose only
looked at her and cried louder.

Mrs. MacNally ran back out to Maureen and Alfie. Now the drips were coming from lots of different places, splash, splash, splash!

"We ought to turn the water off at the main," said Maureen, "but I don't know how you do it. I think I'd better fetch Dad."

While she was gone, Mrs. MacNally mopped
and mopped and emptied brimming bowls,
and in between mopping and emptying, she ran
to try to comfort Annie Rose. But Annie Rose
went on crying and crying. The drips came
faster and faster.

Now there were a lot of puddles on the floor. Alfie paddled in them for a while. It was fun, but the water was very cold. He thought that soon perhaps the whole street would be covered with water, and they would all have to float away in a boat, like Noah's ark.

Soon Maureen came running
upstairs with Mr. MacNally,
wearing his bedroom slippers,
close behind her.

"What's all this, then?" said Mr.
MacNally, looking at all the water
pouring down.

He put his head around the bedroom door. He and Annie Rose were old friends.

"Dear, dear, what's all this?" he said in a very kind voice.

Then he went downstairs and found a valve under the stairs and turned it off, just like that.

"So *that's* where it is," said Maureen.

Then the water stopped pouring down
through the ceiling, splash! splash! splash! and
became a drip-drip, drip-drip, drip-drip,

and then a drip. . . drip. . . drip. . . drip. . .
and then it stopped altogether.

"Oh, thank goodness for that!" said Mrs. MacNally.

"I'll know how to do it next time," said Maureen.

But Annie Rose was still crying.

Alfie went into the bedroom to see if he could cheer her up. Tears were rolling down her cheeks and soaking into her blanket.

"Don't cry, Annie Rose," said Alfie. He put his hand through the bars of her crib and patted her very gently, as he had seen Mom do sometimes.

Annie Rose still wore diapers at night.

"Annie Rose is wet," Alfie told everyone. "And her bed's wet too. I expect that's why she's crying."

"Why, so she is, poor little mite!" said Mrs. MacNally.

When Annie Rose was dry and comfortable again, Mrs. MacNally put her on the living-room sofa with Alfie and tucked a quilt around them. Then she gave them each a cookie.

Annie Rose was quite cheerful now. She got very friendly with Mr. MacNally, and he let her play a game with him, taking off his glasses and putting them on again. Then she sucked her thumb and leaned up against Alfie, and Alfie leaned up against her. When Mom and Dad came home, they were both fast asleep.

The next morning Mom told Alfie not to turn on the taps until the plumber had come to fix the burst pipe.

Alfie didn't mind not having to wash. He'd had enough water the evening before to last for a long time.